Brontorina

JAMES HOWE

illustrated by RANDY CECIL

templar publishing

A TEMPLAR BOOK

First published in the UK in 2010 by Templar Publishing,
an imprint of The Templar Company Limited,
The Granary, North Street, Dorking, RH4 1DN, UK
www.templarco.co.uk

Originally published in 2010 in the USA by Candlewick Press,
99 Dover Street, Somerville, Massachusetts 02144
www.candlewick.com

1 3 5 7 9 10 8 6 4 2

ISBN 978 1 84877 035 5

Printed in China

For Mark,
a dancer in his heart
J.H.

For Sophie
R.C.

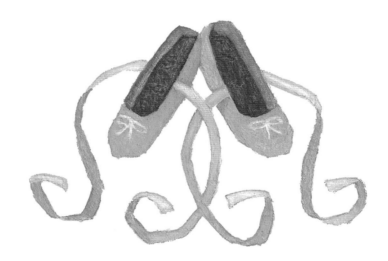

Brontorina had a dream.

"But you are a dinosaur," Madame Lucille
pointed out.

"True," Brontorina replied. "But in my heart
I am a ballerina."

Madame Lucille wondered what to do. She had never had a dinosaur as a student before. Dinosaurs were rather large. And this one certainly did not have the right shoes.

But then she felt Clara and Jack tugging at her skirt. "Oh, please!" they pleaded.

Madame Lucille looked into the dinosaur's eyes.
"What is your name, my dear?"

"Brontorina. Brontorina Apatosaurus. I even
sound like a dancer, don't you agree?"

Madame Lucille did agree. How could she not?

"Welcome to Madame Lucille's Dance Academy for Girls and Boys," she said. "Please try not to squash the other dancers."

"Music, Magnolia!" she instructed the academy's piano player.

As Magnolia started to play, Madame Lucille also began to instruct her students.

"What a graceful dancer you are, my dear!" Madame Lucille exclaimed.

Brontorina blushed. "On the outside, I am a dinosaur. But in my heart—"

"You are a ballerina!" cried Clara and Jack.

She still doesn't have the right shoes!

In the weeks that followed…

"Oh, Brontorina!" cried Madame Lucille. "I'm afraid you are too big to be a ballerina. You barely fit in my studio. And how in the world will a male dancer ever lift you over his head?"

"I could do it!" Jack shouted.

"No, my dear," said Madame Lucille with a sigh, "you could not."

A tear fell from Brontorina's eye.
Downcast, she turned to leave.

"Wait!" Clara called out. "Don't go. My mother has been working on a surprise for you all week, Brontorina. She is bringing it today."

"Whatever are you talking about?" Madame Lucille asked Clara.

Just then, Clara's mother appeared at the door.
"You must be Brontorina," she said, holding out
the surprise. "I hope these will fit."

Well, now she has the right shoes.

Brontorina beamed. "They fit perfectly!" she cried.
"I am a ballerina! Or I would be… if only I weren't
so… big."

"Oh, fiddlesticks!" said Madame Lucille. "Why
didn't I see it before? The problem is not that you are
too big. The problem is that my studio is too small."

And so the whole class went off to
look for a studio big enough to hold all
of Brontorina's talent.

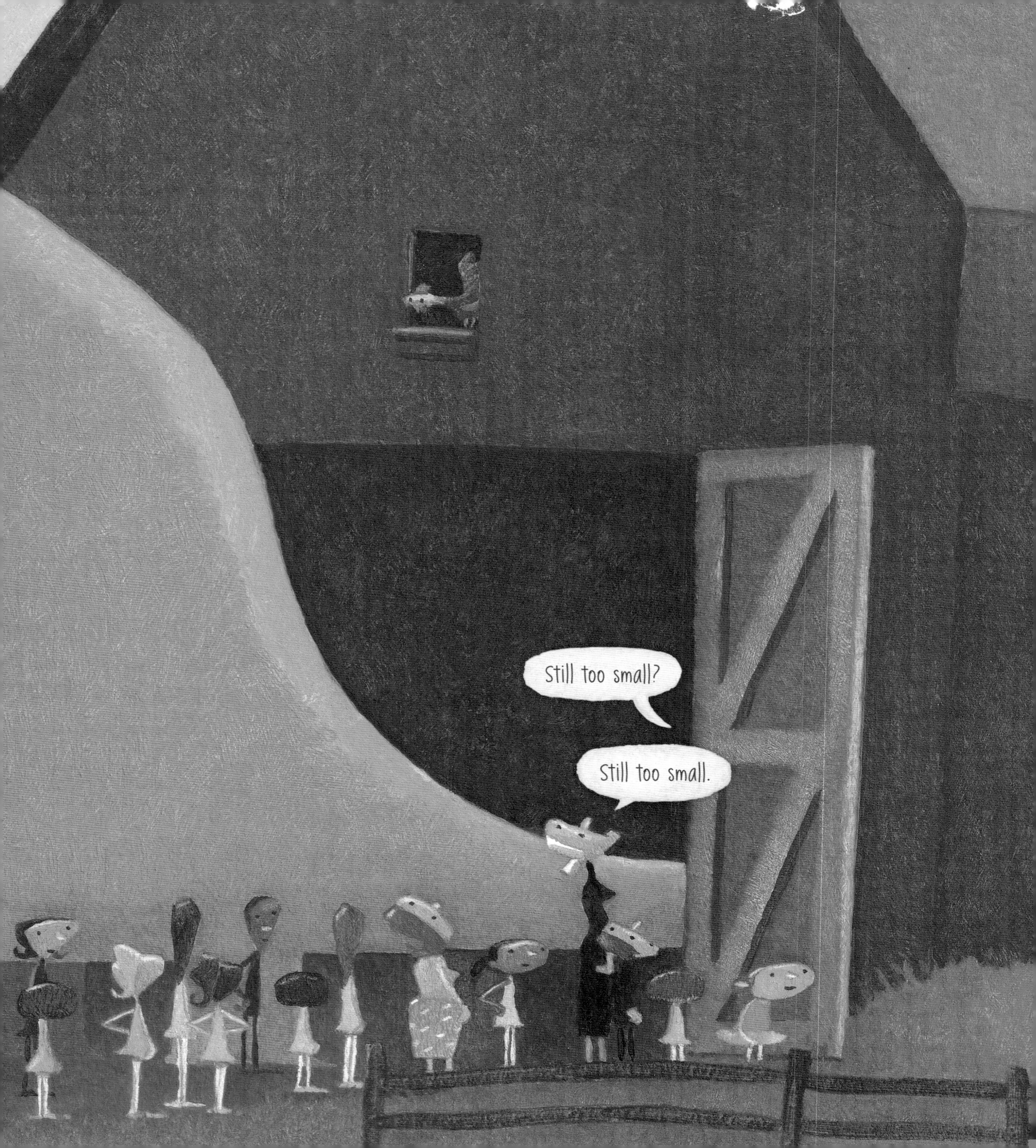
Still too small?
Still too small.

Now Madame Lucille's dance academy had room for everyone.

And it all began with a dream.